Please Mum!

Written by Julie Ellis

Illustrated by Andy Hammond

"Look, buns!
I love buns.
Please Mum, please Mum,
can I have a bun?"

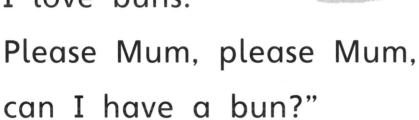

"Sh!" said Mum.

"Now, what did I want?"

"Look, cakes!
I love cakes.
Please Mum, please Mum,
can I have a cake?"

"Sh!" said Mum.

"Now, what did I want?"

"Look, cookies!
I love cookies.
Please Mum, please Mum,
can I have a cookie?"

"Sh-sh!" said Mum.

"Now, what did I want?"

"**PLEASE**, Mum! **PLEASE**, Mum!"

"Oh, all right," said Mum.

"Please can I have some bread..."

...**and** a bun, **and** a cake,
and a cookie."